mcc

Dear Parent.
Your child's lo.. ~, reading starts here!

Every ch~~~~~~~~~~~~~ ..ay and at his or her own
speed. S~ **This book is tc** ...ding levels and read
favourite **before ''** ...rs read through each level in
order. Y~ ...~ur young reader improve and become more
confiden ~y encouraging his or her own interests and abilities. From
books your child reads with you to the first books he or she reads
alone, there are I Can Read Books for every stage of reading:

SHARED READING
Basic language, word repetition, and whimsical illustrations,
ideal for sharing with your emergent reader

BEGINNING READING
Short sentences, familiar words, and simple concepts
for children eager to read on their own

READING WITH HELP
Engaging stories, longer sentences, and language play
for developing readers

READING ALONE
Complex plots, challenging vocabulary, and high-interest topics
for the independent reader

ADVANCED READING
Short paragraphs, chapters, and exciting themes
for the perfect bridge to chapter books

I Can Read Books have introduced children to the joy of reading
since 1957. Featuring award-winning authors and illustrators and a
fabulous cast of beloved characters, I Can Read Books set the
standard for beginning readers.

A lifetime of discovery begins with the magical words **"I Can Read!"**

*Visit www.icanread.com for information
on enriching your child's reading experience.*

Meet the Silver Hatch Gang

First published in the UK by HarperCollins Children's Books in 2008
HarperCollins Children's Books is a division of HarperCollins Publishers Ltd.

1 3 5 7 9 10 8 6 4 2

ISBN-13: 978-0-00-727516-8
ISBN-10: 0-00-727516-1

© Chapman Entertainment Limited & David Jenkins 2008
www.roarytheracingcar.com

A CIP catalogue for this title is available from the British Library.

Printed and bound in China

I Can Read!

BEGINNING
1
READING

Meet the
Silver Hatch
Gang

HarperCollins *Children's Books*

This is Roary the Racing Car.

He lives at Silver Hatch Race Track with all of his friends.

Would you like to meet them?

This is Big Chris.

He looks after all of the cars at Silver Hatch.

He also loves to sing!

Maxi is the fastest car
Roary has ever met.
He wins lots of races at Silver Hatch
but he is not always very nice
to the other cars.

Roary thinks it is more important to have friends than win races.

Cici is one of Roary's best friends.
She is a little pink stunt car
and loves to have fun!

This is Marsha the marshall. She is in charge of all the races and rides around on her scooter, Zippee.

Zippee loves zipping around all day!

Drifter comes all the way from Japan and has blue lights underneath. Roary thinks he is the coolest car at the race track.

Tin Top is an American stockcar.

He is covered in bumps

because he has been in so many races.

Tin Top is not a very careful driver!

Flash lives under the race track
and is always causing trouble!
He might be a little bit naughty
but Roary thinks that
Flash is one funny bunny.

Molecom helps Big Chris look after all of the cars in the pit lane.

Molecom can't see anything without his glasses!

Farmer Green lives on the farm.

Big Chris loves to get fresh eggs.

Farmer Green's truck, FB, delivers the eggs and milk to the race track.

Big Chris lives at Silver Hatch in his caravan, Rusty.

Rusty likes to sleep

almost as much as

Big Chris likes to sing!

Plugger works on the race track, towing things for Big Chris.

Dinkie lives in a field by the track and loves to watch the races.

He is Roary's biggest fan.

This is Mr Carburettor.

He owns Silver Hatch race track

and all the cars.

He is very important and travels around in his helicopter, Hellie.

Now you have met
all of Roary's friends,
would you like to watch a race
at Silver Hatch one day?

Race to the finish line with these fun story and activity books.

Big Chris's Big Workout
Can Big Chris beat Marsha round the track?

Flash Flips Out
Roary's racing and Flash is furious!

Roary's First Day
Can Roary make a splash on his first match?

Pole Position Poster Book
Customise the cars with Roary!
48

Big Chris's Race Day Sticker Book
Help Big Chris get Roary ready to race!
40

Roary the Racing Car is out now on DVD!

Rev up R/C Roary to race to victory!

Start your engines with Talking Big Chris!

Go Roary, go-oooo!

Get to

Ligh up

Visit Roary at www.roarytheracingcar.com